Ramona Quimby, Age 8

by
Beverly Cleary

Teacher Guide

Written by
Phyllis A. Green

Note

The Dell Yearling paperback edition of the book published by Dell was used to prepare this guide. The page references may differ in the hardcover or other paperback editions.

Please note: Please assess the appropriateness of this book for the age level and maturity of your students prior to reading and discussing it with your class.

ISBN 1-56137-448-2

To order, contact your local school
supply store, or—

Novel Units, Inc.
P.O. Box 791610
San Antonio, TX 78279

Web site: www.educyberstor.com

Table of Contents

Background 3

Instructional Strategies for a
Ramona Unit 3

Activity Sheets 4

Story Summary 6

About the Author..6

Initiating Activities.......................................7

Nine Chapters...9
  Chapters contain: Plot Summary, Vocabulary
  Words, Discussion Questions, Predictions,
  Supplementary Activities

Concluding Activities...................................22

Vocabulary Activities...................................24

Activity Sheets 31

Skills and Strategies

Thinking
Visualization, brainstorming, synthesis

Comprehension
Predicting, comparison/ contrast

Writing
Description, explanation, narrative, journaling

Vocabulary
Antonyms/synonyms, word mapping, classifying

Listening/Speaking
Discussion, interviewing

Literary Elements
Characterization, protagonist, story elements

Background

Beverly Cleary has written a series of books featuring Ramona, her family, and her friends. These books provide opportunity for a unit of study for grades 3-5, studying a well-developed character and making judgments about growing up.

Instructional Strategies for a Ramona Unit

1. Choose one of the Ramona books for direct reading instruction. Students will then *choose* other Ramona books to read independently. Class idea maps (attribute webs or other graphic organizers) will be used to record ideas from the various Ramona books.

2. Stage a Ramona celebration, an afternoon focused on the Cleary Ramona books. The celebration can start with a Ramona lunch, followed with a variety of Ramona activities:

    - games;
    - songs and music;
    - library favorites;
    - drama;
    - hobbies.

    Each of the categories above will be a planning committee with students chairing and directing the committee whose purpose will be to choose and prepare activities in their category that Ramona has done or would enjoy. A rationale is needed to support choices of activities.

3. Explain why Ramona is a memorable main character. (See page 4 of this guide.) Interview your parents about memorable characters from their reading, especially characters who have appeared in several books.

4. Think about a Ramona movie. (See page 5 of this guide for details on "Your Book Has Been Optioned for the Movies.")

5. Prepare a Ramona time line, including Ramona's antics on one side of the line and typical human behaviors on the other side of the line.

Ramona's antics

Behaviors and expectations for each age

Where's the Protagonist???

1. What does the word "protagonist" mean?

   _____

   _____

2. List your favorite main characters from books you've read.

   _____   _____   _____

   _____   _____   _____

   _____   _____   _____

3. From the list above, describe these characters on a web.

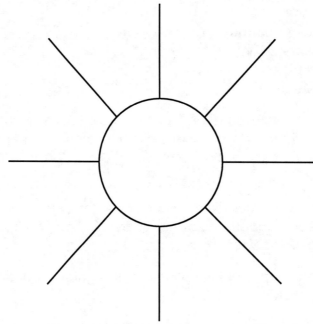

4. Ramona is _____, _____, and _____. The author has described Ramona by giving us (the readers) _____, _____, and _____. Ramona is a well-crafted protagonist because she _____

   _____.

Your Book Has Been Optioned for the Movies

1. You are the casting director. Who are the lead roles, supporting cast, and walk-ons? What kind of characters are they? What actors will fill the roles? How should they look? What acting abilities will they need?

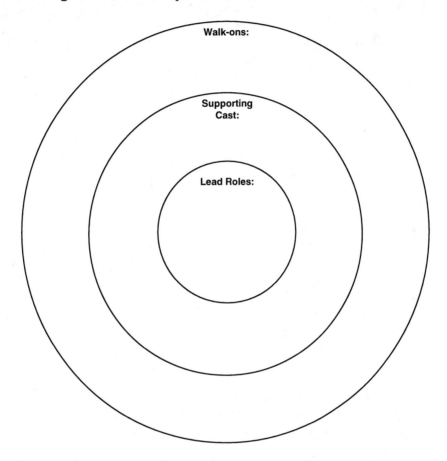

Walk-ons:

Supporting Cast:

Lead Roles:

2. Design costumes for the cast. Explain your choices.

3. Pick the music. Will you need background music only or will you have musical "numbers"?

4. Design the set.

5. Identify and describe the props.

6. What will you title your movie? Why?

Story Summary

Ramona is in Mrs. Whaley's third grade class. Ramona has problems with Mrs. Whaley as well as with her family. Like most third graders, she misunderstands and is misunderstood. Ramona's low point in life is reached the day she throws up in class. This is a funny story which boys and girls enjoy.

About the Author

Beverly Bunn Cleary was born in 1916. When she was two, her mother told her to remember a celebration and bells ringing near her home. Years later she asked about the commotion and was told that it was the end of World War I.

An only child, she was born to a farmer and a school teacher. In her early years, she lived on a farm in Yamhill, Oregon. (Note that her autobiography is entitled *A Girl from Yamhill.*) Hard times forced the family to move to Portland where she started school. Her shy country manner probably contributed to her "passed on trial" promotion to second grade. By third grade, happily, she was an avid reader.

The mother of twins, she earned her B.A. from the University of California, Berkeley. She did library work at the University of Washington. She worked in libraries until 1945 when she began to write children's books full-time.

Her books have won many honors, including the 1984 Newbery Award for *Dear Mr. Henshaw*. *Ramona and Her Father* and *Ramona Quimby, Age 8* were Newbery Honor Books.

Her books include the following:

> *Beezus and Ramona* (Novel Units® guides Available)
> *Dear Mr. Henshaw* (Novel Units® guides Available)
> *Ellen Tebbits* (Novel Units® guides Available)
> *Emily's Runaway Imagination*
> *Fifteen*
> *A Girl from Yamhill: A Memoir* (an adult autobiography)
> *The Growing-Up Feet*
> *Henry and Beezus*
> *Henry and Ribsy*
> *Henry and the Clubhouse* (Novel Units® guides Available)
> *Henry and the Paper Route*
> *Henry Huggins* (Novel Units® guides Available)
> *The Hullabaloo ABC*
> *Janet's Thingamajigs*
> *Jean and Johnny*

The Luckiest Girl
Lucky Chuck
Mitch and Amy
The Mouse and the Motorcycle (Novel Units® guides Available)
Muggie Maggie
Otis Spofford (Novel Units® guides Available)
Ralph S. Mouse (Novel Units® guides Available)
Ramona
Ramona and Her Father (Novel Units® guides Available)
Ramona and Her Mother
Ramona Forever (Novel Units® guides Available)
Ramona the Brave (Novel Units® guides Available)
Ramona the Pest (Novel Units® guides Available)
Ramona's World (Novel Units® guides Available)
The Real Hole
Ribsy (Novel Units® guides Available)
Runaway Ralph (Novel Units® guides Available)
Sister of the Bride
Socks
Strider (Novel Units® guides Available)
Two Dog Biscuits

Initiating Activities

1. Imagine a new student named Ramona Quimby. What would you predict about her? What questions would you want her to answer about herself? Brainstorm answers, recording on a large sheet to display during the novel unit. As the story unfolds, cross off, revise, and change the list.

2. Let's begin this book as if we're going on a trip with a story map. We need the answers to some questions. Using the story map on page 8 to record your answers, consider:

   a) Who is the main character?
   b) Where does the story take place? When does the story take place?
   c) Is the story make-believe or true-to-life?
   d) What is the problem in the story? Does the problem change or are there several problems? **Watch this and maybe we will have to make adjustments to the story map.**

Story Map

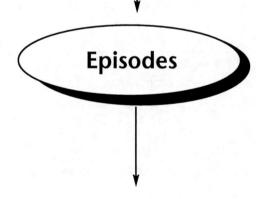

Setting

↓

Problem

↓

Goal

↓

Episodes

↓

Resolution

Characters_____

_____

Time and Place_____

_____

Problem_____

_____

_____

Goal_____

_____

_____

Beginning ——→ Development ——→ Outcome

_____

_____

_____

_____

Resolution_____

_____

_____

_____

3. Collect information about eight-year-olds. Describe the age, including physical characteristics, learning challenges, typical games, typical schooling, likes/dislikes. List your findings on a large chart. As you read the book *Ramona Quimby, Age 8*, decide how typical the main character is.

Chapter 1: "The First Day of School"—Pages 11-36

Plot Summary:
Third grade brings challenges to Ramona—a new teacher, a bus ride, retrieving her pink eraser from Danny, and dealing with her new squeaky, large sandals.

Vocabulary:

quivery 11	swished 13	appreciated 16
responsibility 19	convinced 23	reassuring 24
visor 24	cootie 26	anxious 26
ferocious 27	wedges 28	encumbered 29
fuming 31	erupt 31	astonishment 34
triumphant 34	reprimand 35	cursive 35
curliques 36		

Discussion Questions:
1. How were Ramona, Beezus, and Mr. Quimby alike? *(Page 13, They were all going to start school.)*

2. Why did Mr. Quimby call himself Santa's Little Helper? *(Page 20, Because the temperature in the warehouse where he worked was below zero.)*

3. There are lots of symbols for luck, e.g. horseshoes, rabbit's foot, but what was the symbol for luck that Mr. Quimby gave Ramona? *(page 16, a pink eraser)*

4. Why did Ramona call the boys "Yucky yard apes"? *(Page 29 and 31, it was her name for boys, who always got the best balls, who were always first on the playground, and who chased their soccer balls through hopscotch games.)*

5. Why do you think Yard Ape returned Ramona's eraser? *(Answers vary.)*

6. Ramona has many problems. Keep track of them on a Problem Chart.

Problem	Solution Attempts	Outcomes
	1.	
	2.	
	3.	
	4.	
	5.	

Supplementary Activities:

1. Did the author start the story at an appropriate place? Give reasons for your answer. How does an author title a chapter?

2. What is the mood of Chapter 1? How did the author let the reader know the mood? Give examples from the book.

3. Start an attribute web for Mrs. Whaley. (See pages 11-12 of this guide.)

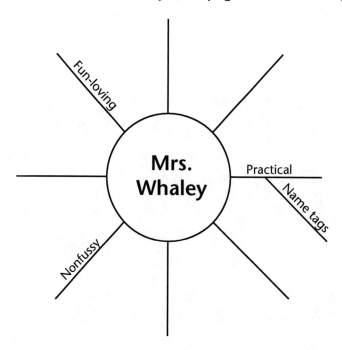

Chapter 2: "At Howie's House"—Pages 37-54

Plot Summary:
Ramona does her part by getting along with Willa Jean at the Kemps' after school, but it's hard to cope with Willa Jean and her dress-up games.

Vocabulary:

horrid 37	dismount 43	impatiently 45
wistfully 46	seized 50	pranced 50
overwhelmed 53	inspiration 53	impressed 53
conspiratorial 54	blissfully 54	

Prediction:
In Chapter 1 we met Howie. What *could* happen to Ramona in this chapter? Will it be something happy or sad? Write your prediction. (See pages 13-14 of this guide.)

Using Character Webs

Attribute Webs are simply a visual representation of a character from the novel. They provide a systematic way for the students to organize and recap the information they have about a particular character. Attribute webs may be used after reading the novel to recapitulate information about a particular character or completed gradually as information unfolds, done individually, or finished as a group project.

One type of character attribute web uses these divisions:

• How a character acts and feels. (How does the character feel in this picture? How would you feel if this happened to you? How do you think the character feels?)

• How a character looks. (Close your eyes and picture the character. Describe him to me.)

• Where a character lives. (Where and when does the character live?)

• How others feel about the character. (How does another specific character feel about our character?)

In group discussion about the student attribute webs and specific characters, the teacher can ask for backup proof from the novel. You can also include inferential thinking.

Attribute webs need not be confined to characters. They may also be used to organize information about a concept, object or place.

Attribute Web

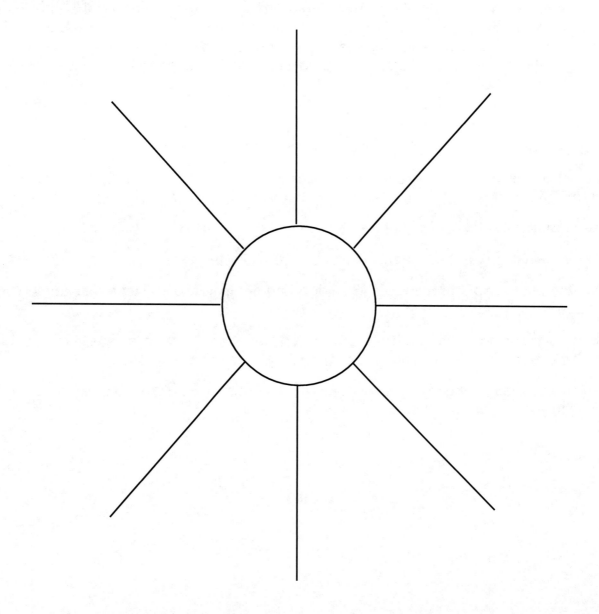

Using Predictions

We all make predictions as we read—little guesses about what will happen next, how the conflict will be resolved, which details given by the author will be important to the plot, which details will help to fill in our sense of a character. Students should be encouraged to predict, to make sensible guesses. As students work on predictions, these discussion questions can be used to guide them: What are some of the ways to predict? What is the process of a sophisticated reader's thinking and predicting? What clues does an author give us to help us in making our predictions? Why are some predictions more likely than others?

A predicting chart is for students to record their predictions. As each subsequent chapter is discussed, you can review and correct previous predictions. This procedure serves to focus on predictions and to review the stories.

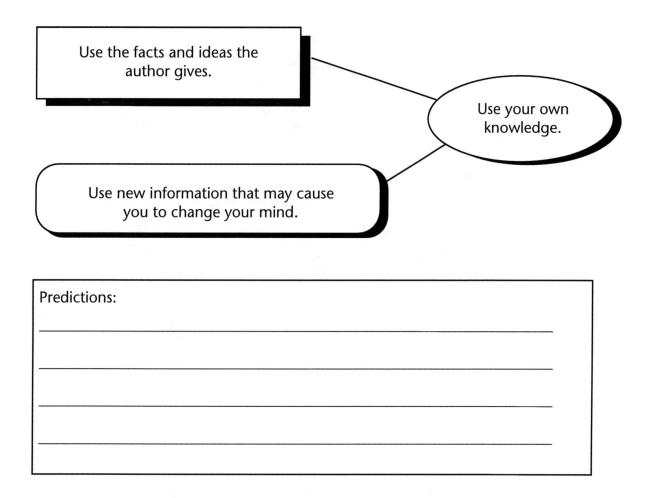

Use the facts and ideas the author gives.

Use your own knowledge.

Use new information that may cause you to change your mind.

Predictions:

_____

_____

_____

_____

© Novel Units, Inc.

13

Prediction Chart

What characters have we met so far?	What is the conflict in the story?	What are your predictions?	Why did you make those predictions?

Discussion Questions:

1. Why was it hard for Ramona to be a Quimby? *(Page 38, Father was tired, in a hurry, or studying; no television.)*

2. Why did Ramona go to Howie's house? *(Page 43, Her mother was working and her father was at school.)*

3. Ramona's parents asked her to "do her part." What did that mean? *(Page 45, Ramona's job in the Quimby family was to get along at the Kemps' with Willa Jean.)*

4. Why did Ramona think she was clever? *(Page 53, She told Willa Jean she had to do Sustained Silent Reading. Willa Jean was impressed by the phrase she did not understand and Ramona didn't have to play with Willa Jean.)*

5. How would you entertain a difficult little girl like Willa Jean if you were in Ramona's shoes? Make a list of suggestions. *(Answers vary.)*

Supplementary Activities:

1. Consider the book's illustrations. Alan Tiegreen has provided illustrations for several Ramona books. (See bibliography listing on pages 6-7.) Look at the illustrations in *Ramona Quimby, Age 8* as well as at least one other Tiegreen book. Then discuss these questions:

   a) What does Tiegreen emphasize in his illustrations?
   b) How does he use line, space, color?

2. What are your experiences with Silent Sustained Reading? Collect your ideas on a web.

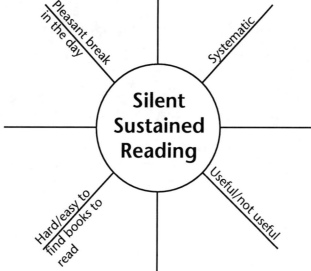

3. Collect a class list of great books for Silent Sustained Reading.

Chapter 3: "The Hard-Boiled Egg"—Pages 55-73

Plot Summary:
Ramona joins the class with a hard-boiled egg in her lunch. The only difference is that she has, in error, a raw egg and she ends up with a major mess in her hair.

Vocabulary:

flurried 55	larvae 57	commotion 62
aloof 64	snuffled 65	humiliation 66
nuisance 68	reluctantly 70	

Prediction:
Do any of you know how to make a hard-boiled egg? What is a fad? What could a hard-boiled egg fad be? Make a guess.

Discussion Questions:
1. Why would Ramona take a hard-boiled egg for lunch if she didn't like to eat them? *(Page 56, Because everyone else was doing it.)* Have you ever done anything because everyone else was doing it.

2. How did you feel when you read about Ramona cracking the raw egg on her head? What would you have done? *(Answers vary.)*

3. What did Mrs. Whaley say about Ramona? How do you think Ramona felt about Mrs. Whaley? *(Page 68, "I hear my little show-off came in with egg in her hair...what a nuisance.")*

4. Why did Ramona feel "like a real person again" after deciding to continue using a printed Q? *(Page 73, Answers vary, but include the idea of personal control.)*

Supplementary Activities:
1. Make a list of characteristics you think a teacher should have. Ask some friends/ classmates to read your list and sign their name when they agree with you.

2. "Egg in her hair" was an embarrassing time for Ramona. What makes someone embarrassed? Answer in a short paragraph, using examples from this book as well as other books.

Chapter 4: "The Quimbys' Quarrel"—Pages 74-90

Plot Summary:
The Quimbys disagree about eating tongue.

Vocabulary:

rueful 78	emerged 79	squishy 79
seized 80	nutritious 83	ridiculous 83
defiant 84	unrelenting 84	suppressed 84
sulky 84	plight 85	scowled 88
dismal 89		

Discussion Questions:

1. Make attribute webs about Mr. and Mrs. Quimby. What kind of parents were they?

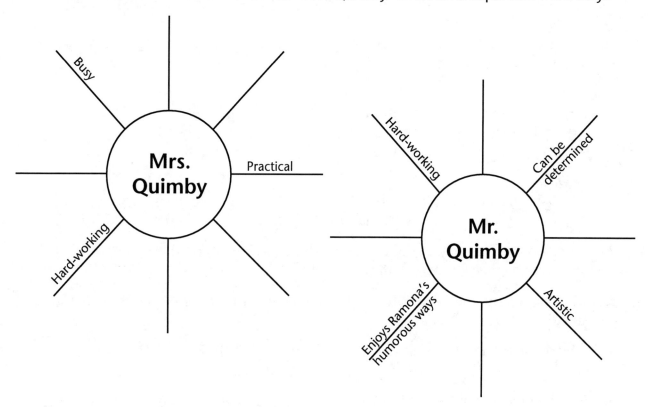

2. Why didn't Ramona and Beezus like dinner? Is there some food that you just cannot eat? *(Page 81, The meat was tongue.)*

3. What were the girls going to try to do to get their parents to forget about their punishment? *(page 89, try to be extra good, get up without being called, avoid arguing, compliment Mother on French toast, clean rooms, get ready for Sunday School)*

Supplementary Activities:
1. Discussion: Families and family members have many different reasons for irritation. With a small group, brainstorm a listing of these various irritations. Then talk about some ways to overcome the irritations. Summarize your ideas in a short paragraph.

2. How do parents teach their children table manners? Reread Ramona's experiences with table manners on page 80 and discuss your own experiences. In a short paragraph tell how you'd teach children table manners.

Chapter 5: "The Extra-good Sunday"—Pages 91-108

Plot Summary:
Ramona and Beezus manage to cook an edible Sunday dinner. Mr. and Mrs. Quimby wash the dishes and clean up the kitchen.

Vocabulary:

complimented 91	yoghurt 94	frantically 95
highlighted 99	hurled 100	calamity 101
anxiety 105	edible 105	suppressed 105

Discussion Questions:
1. What did the girls cook for supper? *(chicken, corn bread, rice, peas)* What can you cook? If your mother and father had told you to get supper, what would you fix?

2. What did the girls play tug-of-war with? Have you ever done something this disgusting? *(page 97, chicken thighs)*

3. Was this chapter funny? Why were the characters believable? How did the author create the chapter's mood?

4. Why did Ramona feel better that Yard Ape had called her Egghead? *(Page 107, Her father explained Egghead was slang for a very smart person.)*

5. How were Ramona's feelings toward Yard Ape changed from the beginning of the book? *(Answers vary.)*

Supplementary Activities:
1. Make two or three lists:

   a) Things for parents only to decide.
   b) Responsibilities parents must carry out.
   c) Things a person your age can decide better for himself.

   Share your lists with a classmate. Do you have some of the same things on your lists?

2. Interview some adults to find out how one gets a meal cooked and finished at the right time. Summarize your answers in a short paragraph.

3. Try cooking a meal for your family. Record your experiences and compare to the adventure of Beezus and Ramona.

4. Try drawing your foot as Mr. Quimby did.

Chapter 6: "Supernuisance"—Pages 109-126

Plot Summary:
Ramona throws up in class.

Vocabulary:

sober 109	dawdle 110	scant 111
plodded 113	insert 114	welled 115
motioned 118	quavered 119	pediatrician 124
reassuring 125		

Discussion Questions:
1. What happened that made Ramona feel she really was a nuisance? *(Page 115, She threw up in class.)*

2. Why did Ramona think she'd still feel terrible in the morning? *(Page 125, Her stomach might feel better, but the rest of her world would be terrible...her teacher thought she was a nuisance and she wondered what nickname Yard Ape would give her this time.)*

Supplementary Activities:
1. Beverly Cleary uses a variety of words to describe how Ramona walks. Search through the book for these descriptions. Write the words on 3 x 5 cards. Students draw cards from among the 3 x 5 cards to act out (e.g., dawdle, plodded).

2. Ramona's emotions change according to her adventures and reactions in each chapter. Divide a paper into eight parts to record Ramona's feelings chapter by chapter with an illustration and a one word summary.

Chapter 7: "The Patient"—Pages 127-144

Plot Summary:
Ramona recuperates from the flu at home.

Vocabulary:

consideration 128	receptionist 130	indignant 133
arthritic 134	kneaded 134	indigestion 134
transmission 142	exhausted 144	

Discussion Questions:
1. How did Ramona's mother know that Ramona was getting better? *(Page 132, "I can tell you're beginning to get well when you act like a wounded tiger.")* What does the phrase mean? *(Answers vary, but may include notion of crankiness.)*

2. Why was Yard Ape's get well letter special? *(Pages 138-139, "Dear Superfoot. Get well or I will eat your eraser." Ramona smiled because his letter showed he liked her.)*

Supplementary Activities:
1. Write a postcard to Yard Ape telling him why you like his get well card and how much you appreciated it. Remember there is not much room on a postcard.

2. What do you want when you're a patient?

3. Reread Cleary's word picture of Ramona's cheer-up picture from her father on pages 128 and 129. Draw your own picture.

Chapter 8: "Ramona's Book Report"—Pages 145-161

Plot Summary:
Ramona's book report assignment, to sell her book, is troublesome for her because she considers the book medium-boring. After a humorous TV commercial book report, Ramona confronts Mrs. Whaley about calling Ramona a nuisance.

Vocabulary:

installed 145	affectionate 148	accuracy 149
interrupted 149	inspiration 152	beckoned 155
thrive 156	flustered 156	suppressing 156
desperately 156	affectionately 159	

Discussion Questions:
1. What does creative mean? *(Answers vary.)* Ramona was creative in her commercial for the book report on *The Left-Behind Cat*. Can you make suggestions for a creative book report on *Ramona Quimby, Age 8*?

2. Why was this chapter funny? *(Answers vary.)*

3. Do you think Ramona felt better about Mrs. Whaley after their private talk? Explain your reason.

Supplementary Activities:
1. Choose a way to explain creativity—a word map, a graphic (attribute web or other design map of your own), drawing, oral answer, or quotations. Include your work in a class portfolio on creativity.

2. Interview class members about their favorite commercial slogan. Display some of the slogans on a bulletin board. Choose a favorite to illustrate.

3. What books would Ramona like to read? Start a class list and then use 3 x 5 cards for students to provide book reviews and recommendations for classmates.

Chapter 9: "Rainy Sunday"—Pages 162-190

Plot Summary:
The Quimby Family's Sunday grumpiness is dispelled when Mr. Quimby invites them out for Whopperburgers. A lonely man pays their bill because he thinks they're a nice family. Ramona agrees.

Vocabulary:

dismal 162	smudge 163	sullenly 164
yowled 164	flounced 167	cognitive 171
gnawing 172	balked 176	seething 180
curdled 188		

Discussion Questions:
1. Ramona had lots of worries about her family, especially her father. How did Ramona help? Do you worry about your family? How do you help? *(Pages 185-186, She was a member of a nice sticking-together family and she was old enough to be depended upon so she could ignore a lot of things.)*

2. What happened at the restaurant that made the Quimbys realize what a nice family they really were? *(Page 186, The lonely gentleman paid for the Quimbys' dinner because they were such a nice family and he missed his children and grandchildren.)*

3. What did it mean on page 188 that Ramona's niceness curdled? *(It turned bad just as milk curdles.)*

4. How was Ramona going to try harder to help the family? *(Page 190, She would try reading SSR books to Willa Jean. She would get along better with Mrs. Whaley.)*

Concluding Activities

1. Choose a favorite chapter to make a multiple panel cartoon of the action.

2. Celebrate your learning by choosing one of the following:

   a) With a group, present Readers Theatre of your favorite incident from the book.
   b) Create a Ramona game.
   c) Complete a story map twice—once summarizing this book and once detailing a sequel.
   d) Create an advertisement for a "set" of Ramona books.
   e) Write a letter to Ramona.
   f) Do another activity of your choice.

3. Create a Ramona cube. On each face put a descriptive word or label to introduce Ramona. Choose three small objects that would be special to Ramona to put inside a cube. (See page 23 of this guide.)

4. What is the theme of the book? What values did Cleary support in this book? Defend your choice in a short paragraph.

5. Choose a chapter of *Ramona Quimby, Age 8*. Divide paper into four squares and then draw pictures to show the sequence of actions. Label the chapter. Each child should sign his work as an artist.

6. Character Hanging:

   a) Make a paper head of Ramona or use a small paper plate. Glue on hair—yarn. Make eyes, mouth and nose.
   b) Cut a few circles out of paper.
   c) On each circle write something about Ramona, e.g. all the unusual things she does; members of her family, the funniest incident.
   d) Punch holes in the head and the top and bottom of each circle.
   e) Connect the head and circles with pieces of yarn.

7. Plan a Ramona celebration for a third grade class in your building. Cooperative student groups will be responsible for:

   a) Invitations;
   b) Ramona badge for each third-grader;
   c) Entertainment;
   d) Short readings/dialogue dramatizations from the book.

Character Cube

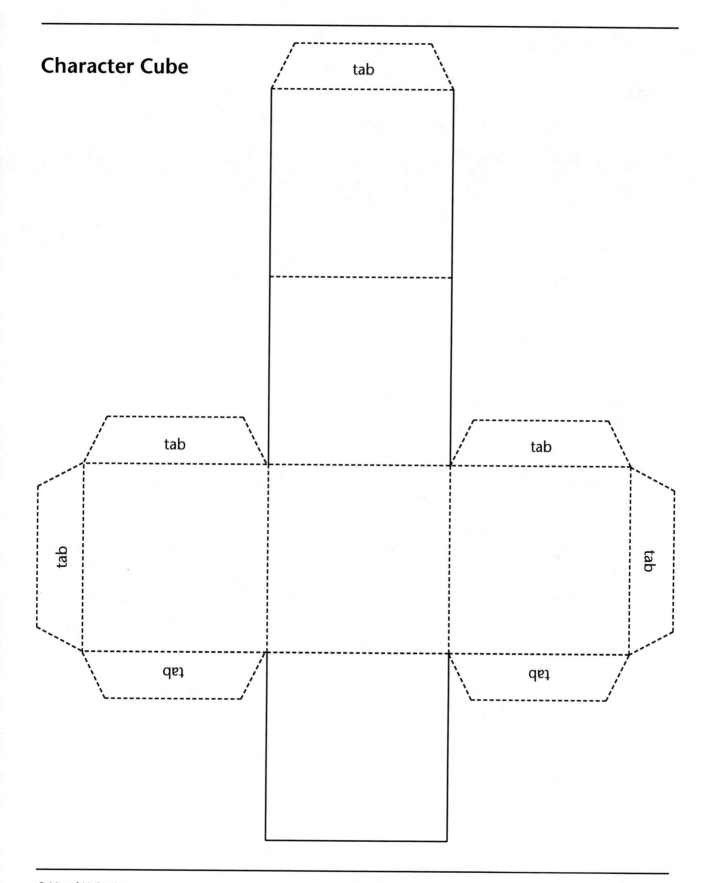

Vocabulary Activities

1. Develop word maps. Use color to distinguish antonyms, synonyms, etc.

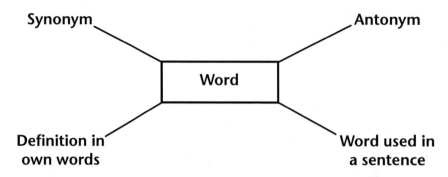

Synonym   Antonym

Word

Definition in   Word used in
own words   a sentence

2. Crossword Puzzles: Have students use vocabulary words from the chapter to make crossword puzzles on graph paper. They should write a question for each word and develop an answer sheet. The teacher will check and then distribute the puzzles to other students to work out in their free time.

3. One student picks a word from the vocabulary list or cards. Another student has ten (or five) questions to discover the word and give the definition.

4. List vocabulary words on large sheets of paper. Leave space for students to a) illustrate the meaning next to each word; b) list a memory device to remember the word.

5. List the vocabulary words on the board or on a sheet of paper in the form of a table. Pronounce the words. Ask the students to rate their knowledge of each of the words (as a group, in cooperative groups or individually).

I Can Define	I Have Heard/Seen	I Don't Know
Words		

6. Provide vocabulary challenge words in context. Ask students to "guess" at the meaning from context, asking why for each guess. Generate a listing of the "why answers" to teach context clues.

7. Select ten words. Write only every other letter and a synonym or definition. Exchange student papers. Example: a_o_a (aroma).

8. Using the vocabulary cards on pages 26-30, laminated or attached to 3 x 5 cards:

   a) Word Sort:

   > I Can Say
   > I Know What It Means
   > I Do Not Know

   b) Word Sort:

   > Action
   > Things
   > Places
   > Names

   c) I am thinking of a word that:

   > Has a long a sound;
   > begins with the same sound as Pat;
   > means _____;
   > is a synonym of _____.

9. Use the vocabulary spinner to explore vocabulary words.

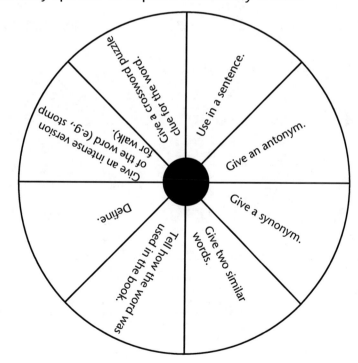

quivery	swished	appreciated
responsibility	convinced	reassuring
visor	cootie	anxious
ferocious	wedges	encumbered
fuming	erupt	astonishment
triumphant	reprimand	cursive
curliques	horrid	dismount
impatiently	wistfully	seized

pranced	overwhelmed	inspiration
impressed	conspiratorial	blissfully
flurried	larvae	commotion
aloof	snuffled	humiliation
nuisance	reluctantly	rueful
emerged	squishy	seized
nutritious	ridiculous	defiant
unrelenting	suppressed	sulky

plight	scowled	dismal
complimented	yoghurt	frantically
highlighted	hurled	calamity
anxiety	edible	suppressed
sober	dawdle	scant
plodded	insert	welled
motioned	quavered	pediatrician
reassuring	consideration	receptionist

indignant	arthritic	kneaded
indigestion	transmission	exhausted
installed	affectionate	accuracy
interrupted	inspiration	beckoned
thrive	flustered	suppressing
desperately	affectionately	dismal
smudge	sullenly	yowled
flounced	cognitive	gnawing

balked	seething	curdled

Activity Sheet

Yard Ape calls Ramona Bigfoot. Think of ten other nicknames for Ramona. List them on the foot. Circle your favorite nickname. Your teacher will redistribute your sheet to another student to write a description of Ramona with your nickname.

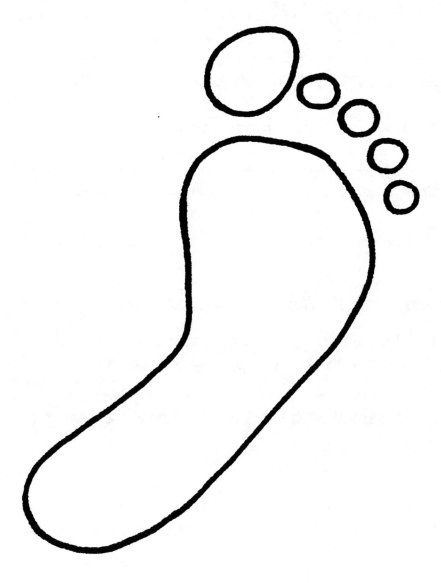

© Novel Units, Inc.

31

Family Writing

(Included here is a selection of writing prompts focusing on the family. The prompts can be used for daily journal writing, as summarizing writing assignments, or as choices for students to build on the themes in the book.)

The Quimby family isn't a typical American family...

My grandmother compares to Howie's grandmother...

My sister and I are just like Beezus and Ramona.

It's hard to be the oldest child/youngest child/ middle child/part of a large family.

I like my family because...

I like the Quimbys because...